# Jake Drake

## BULLY BUSTER

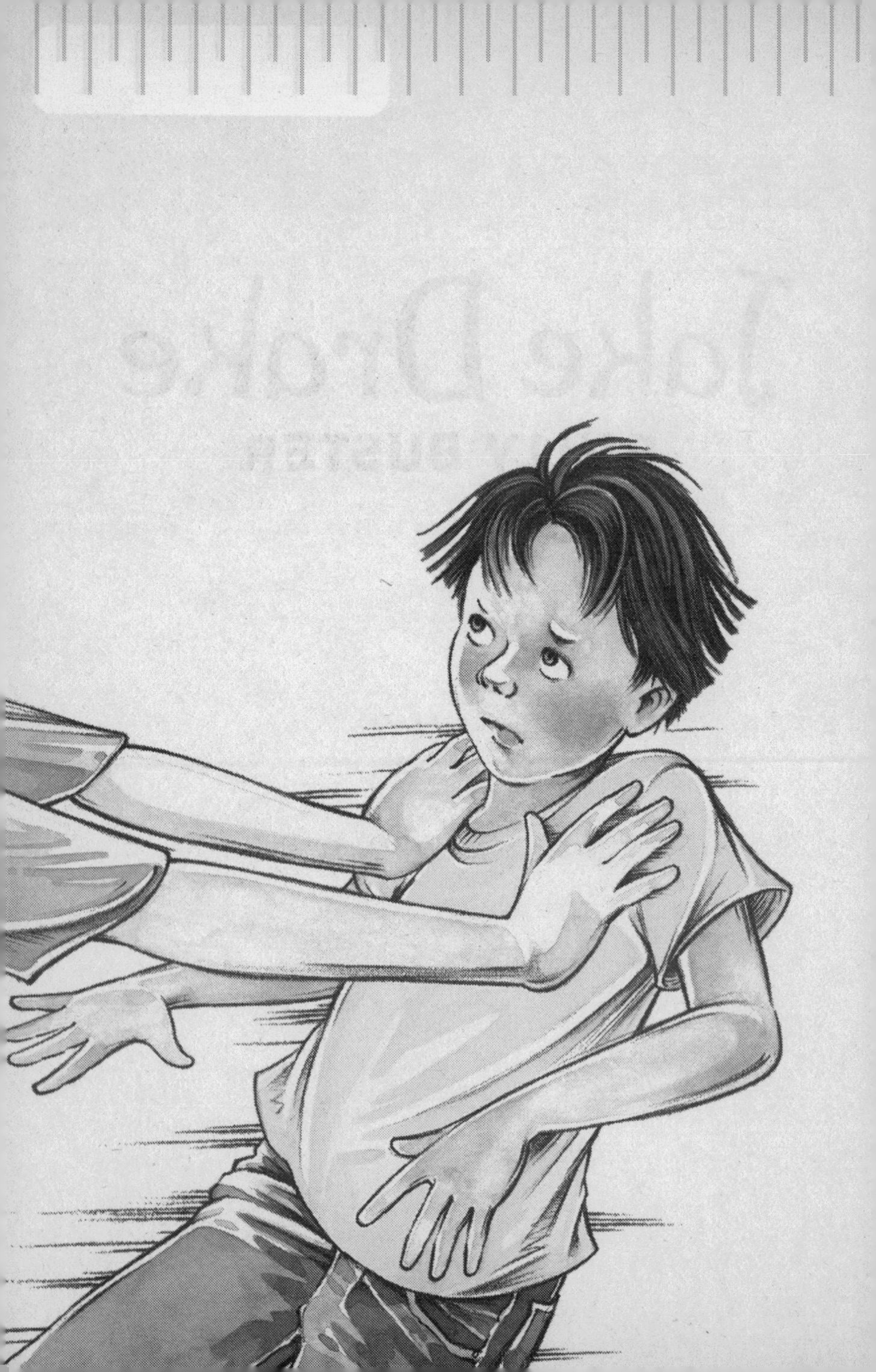

Andrew Clements

# Jake Drake

## BULLY BUSTER

Cover illustration by Marla Frazee

Interior illustrations by Janet Pedersen

ALADDIN PAPERBACKS
New York London Toronto Sydney

**To Kathy, Mary, and Frank Despres**
**in appreciation of their loving, dedicated service**
**to the children of Westborough**

ALADDIN PAPERBACKS
An imprint of Simon & Schuster Children's Publishing Division
1230 Avenue of the Americas, New York, NY 10020

Also available in a Simon & Schuster Books for Young Readers
hardcover edition.
The text of this book was set in Century ITC.
The illustrations were rendered in pen and ink.
Manufactured in the United States of America
First Aladdin Paperbacks edition February 2001
This Aladdin Paperbacks edition June 2007
8 10 9
The Library of Congress has cataloged the hardcover edition as follows:
Clements, Andrew
Jake Drake, bully buster / Andrew Clements ; illustrated by Amanda Harvey
p. cm.
Summary: Fourth-grader Jake Drake relates how he comes to terms with
SuperBully Link Baxter, especially after they are assigned to be
partners on a class project.
ISBN-13: 978-0-689-83917-7 (hc.)
ISBN-10: 0-689-83917-0 (hc.)
[1. Bullying—Juvenile fiction. 2. Bullies—Fiction. 3. Interpersonal relations—
Fiction. 4. Schools—Fiction.]
PZ7.C59118 Jaj 2001
[Fic] 21—lcac
2001270870
ISBN-13: 978-1-4169-3933-7 (pbk.)
ISBN-10: 1-4169-3933-4 (pbk.)

# Contents

## CHAPTER ONE

# Bully-Magnet

I'm Jake—Jake Drake. I'm in fourth grade. Which is my best grade so far. I've got a man teacher this year, Mr. Thompson. He's pretty old, but he's not mean. And he likes the same kinds of books I do. Adventure stories, books about volcanoes and jungles and the ocean, joke books, Calvin and Hobbes—stuff like that.

But there is one thing about Mr. Thompson that's weird. Pete was the first to see it. Which makes sense. Pete is a science kid. He collects bugs and fossils and plants, and he knows all their names, and he's maybe the smartest kid in the school.

After about two weeks of school, Pete pointed at Mr. Thompson. Then he whispered, "He's wearing those pants again."

"Which pants?" I said.

"*Those* pants," Pete said. "The same pants he wore yesterday and the day before and the day before that. I think he wears the same pants *every* day."

"No way," I said. "He probably has a lot of pants that are the same, that's all."

So Pete said, "I'm going to test my theory."

See what I mean? That's how science kids are.

That afternoon we had read-aloud time on the rug, and Mr. Thompson sat in a beanbag chair. Pete sat right next to Mr. Thompson and a little behind him. Mr. Thompson started reading, and he got to the part when the Swiss Family Robinson wrecks their ship.

All the other kids were looking at Mr. Thompson's face or at the ceiling or somewhere. I was watching Pete.

Pete pulled his hand out of his pocket. His

hand went behind Mr. Thompson's foot, just for a second, and then back to his pocket. And then Pete sat and listened like everyone else.

When reading was over, I got next to Pete and whispered, "What did you do?"

Pete grinned and pulled something out of his pocket. It was a little black marker, the kind that doesn't wash out.

I got behind Mr. Thompson and looked down. On the right leg of his pants, on the back of his cuff, was a tiny black spot.

So that's how we found out that Mr. Thompson really has two pairs of pants. Every Thursday he wears tan pants that are just like the other pair, but they don't have the little black spot and they look a little newer. Pete's theory is that Thursday must be laundry day at Mr. Thompson's house. Because every Friday, we can see the little spot again.

My best friend is Phil Willis. Everyone calls him Willie. Willie isn't in my class this year. We have gym class and music class and art class together, but for the rest of the time Willie has Mrs. Steele.

I'm glad I have Mr. Thompson. I mean, Mrs. Steele is okay, but Willie has a lot more homework than I do. Also, Mrs. Steele is a spelling nut. And a math nut. And a social studies nut. I guess she's a nut about everything. That's why Willie's favorite class this year is gym.

Like I said, I'm in fourth grade. That means I've been going to school for five years now. And if you count the two years I went to Miss Lulu's Dainty Diaper Day Care Center, plus one year of preschool, then it's more like eight years. Eight years of school.

So here's what I can't figure out. If everybody who works at school is so smart, how come they can't get rid of the bullies? How come when it comes to bullies, kids are mostly on their own?

Because every year, it's the same thing. Bullies.

Here's what I mean. Okay, it was way back when I was three. I was at Miss Lulu's Day Care. It was the middle of the morning on my second day, and I was standing in line for milk and cookies. And this kid with a runny nose and baggy overalls cut right in front of me.

I didn't say anything because I didn't know any better. Remember, I was only three back then. For all I knew, kids with runny noses got to go first.

So I took my cookies and my milk and sat down at a table. Nose Boy sat down across from me. I smiled at him and took a drink of my milk.

And what did he do? He reached over and grabbed both my cookies. Before I could swallow my milk, he took a big slobbery bite from each one. Then he put them back on my napkin. And then he smiled at me.

I looked at the stuff coming out of his nose. Then I looked at my cookies. And then I turned my head to look for Miss Lulu.

She was still handing out goodies. A crime had taken place, but Miss Lulu was busy.

So I reached over real fast and took *his* cookies. But then I looked down. Nose Boy had already taken a bite out of them, too.

He smiled again, and I could see the crumbs and chocolate chips stuck in his teeth. So I thought to myself, *Who needs a snack anyway?* I slid his cookies back across the table, drank the rest of my milk, and went outside to play.

Three minutes later I was on a swing, just trying to get it going. And somebody grabbed the chain. That's right—it was Nose Boy again.

He snuffled a little and said, "Mine." Nose Boy wasn't much of a talker.

Then I said something like, "I got here first." That was a mistake. The first rule of dealing with a bully is: Never try to tell him why he's wrong. Bullies don't like that.

He yanked hard on the chain and said, "No! Mine!"

I looked around, and Miss Lulu was on the other side of the playground. Then Nose Boy jerked on the chain again, so I got off the swing.

Nose Boy was my first bully. And for the next four years, I was a bully-magnet.

In preschool it was Mike Rada. I called him Destructo. Blocks, LEGOs, Popsicle sticks, crayons, and paper—no matter what I made or what it was made out of, Destructo tore it to bits.

In kindergarten it was Kenny Russell. Kenny

was King Bump. There are a lot of times every day when a bump or a shove can be bad. Like if you're standing next to a puddle at the bus stop. Or when you're drinking a carton of chocolate milk, or maybe when you're working on a painting. If there was a bumpable moment, King Bump was there, all through kindergarten.

In first grade my main bully was Jack Lerner, also known as The Fist. Jack never actually hit me. He just hit things close to me. Like my lunch bag. Like every day. A big fist does a very bad thing to a Wonder Bread sandwich. And I learned real fast not to bring any little containers of pudding. All during first grade I ate cookie crumbs for dessert.

So that was me. I was Jake Drake, the bully-magnet. It was like all the bullies got together to choose their favorite target. Every bully for miles around seemed to know that I was the perfect kid to pick on. And I think I finally figured out why they all liked me so much.

For one thing, bullies need a kid who's just the right size. If the kid is too big, then there

might be a fight someday. Bullies don't like to fight. And if the kid is too small, then the bullying is too easy. There's no challenge.

Another thing about me that bullies like is that I don't have a big brother, or even a big sister. I just have Abby, and she's two years younger than me. Bullies figure out stuff like that right away.

And bullies can tell that I'm not the kind of kid who runs to tell the teacher all my problems. Whiny tattletales make bad bully-bait.

Also, I think I look kind of brainy. Most bullies don't seem so smart, and when they see a kid who looks like he is, something inside a bully says, "Oh, yeah? Well, now you've got to deal with *me*, smart guy!"

And I guess I am a smart guy, because I *am* good at thinking. And because I'm a good thinker, I finally learned what to do about bullies. But I didn't figure all this out at once. It took me four long years. It took having to deal with Nose Boy, and then Destructo, and King Bump, and The Fist.

It also took being picked on by a Certified, Grade A, SuperBully. Which is what happened back when I was in second grade. That's the year I became Jake Drake, Bully Buster.

## CHAPTER TWO

# SuperBully

Second grade started out great. My mom and dad had asked for me to be in Mrs. Brattle's class. They told me she was the best teacher at Despres Elementary School. She smiled a lot, and there wasn't any homework, and there was a lot of neat stuff all over her room, so I was happy she was my teacher.

Phil Willis had Mrs. Brattle, too. Willie and I were already best friends back in second grade, and we had fun every day. We sat at the same group of tables. We were reading partners. We ate lunch together every day, and we always goofed around during recess. We didn't ride the same bus, but after school sometimes I went to his house, and sometimes he came over to mine.

Best of all, Mrs. Brattle's class had zero bullies. Not one. It was great. I still had to be careful at lunchtime and out on the playground, but most of the time my life was bully-free.

Then, right before Halloween, a new kid moved to town. The minute he walked into Mrs. Brattle's room, I knew I was in trouble.

Mrs. Brattle said, "Class, we have a new student today. His name is Link Baxter."

She kept talking, and we all looked at the new kid. I could see he was kind of tall for a second grader. He had brown hair and a pointy nose and long arms with big hands.

Link Baxter stood there and started looking around the room at all of us, too. When he came to me, he stopped. I looked into his face and I saw that Link Baxter had beady little eyes—bully-eyes. And Link saw me seeing this. And then he smiled at me.

It was not a nice smile.

Then Mrs. Brattle, this lady who was supposed to be such a great teacher, what did she do? She put Link at the same group of desks with me and Willie.

Right away Willie whispered, "Hi. I'm Phil, but really I'm Willie. That's my nickname."

You see, Willie has never had any trouble with bullies, mostly because he's too small. He's a nice kid and he minds his own business, and bullies don't even seem to notice him.

So Link smiled at Willie and said, "Hi."

Then Willie pointed at me and said, "This is Jake."

Link Baxter pointed his beady eyes at me and smiled that bully-smile again. And he said, "Jake. Okay."

I tried to smile and nod at him, but I know I looked kind of spooked, because I *was* spooked. And Link could see I was spooked. And he liked it. And that's when I knew I was in big bully-trouble.

Link was only eight years old, just like me. But I could tell right from the start that Link had big plans. He wanted to be the MVP on the Bully

All-Star team. He wanted to make it into the Bullies Hall of Fame. And me, Jake Drake, *I* was his new project.

On that first day when Link came to my class, we practiced handwriting. Mrs. Brattle passed out some lined white paper. We had to write six sentences very, very neatly. Handwriting practice was the only time we could use a pen instead of a pencil.

I loved using my pen. It was made of bright red plastic, and it had black ink. There was a little button on the side. When I pushed the button, the pen went *click*, and the top popped up.

So I was in the middle of my fifth sentence, almost done. The pen was gliding over the smooth paper. My handwriting looked great.

Then Link gave his desk a quick shake. My desk was touching his desk, so my pen went jerking all over. My paper was a mess.

I looked over at Link, and he smiled. Then he whispered, "Nice pen."

So I went up to Mrs. Brattle and got a new piece of paper. I started copying my sentences

again. But now I watched Link all the time to be sure he didn't shake his desk again. I was so nervous that I messed up two more pieces of paper all by myself. And Link didn't make a move.

So I settled down. I was on the very last sentence. Mrs. Brattle was helping a kid at the back of the room. So Link reached over real fast and flicked my ear. Not hard, just enough to make me jump. My pen skidded, and my paper was a mess all over again.

You see, Link was no ordinary bully. Any big kid can push a little kid around. That's one kind of bullying. But this was different. Link Baxter, well . . . he got inside my head—and it only took him twenty minutes. No doubt about it. This was a bully with real talent.

So there I was, asking Mrs. Brattle for my fifth piece of paper, and she said, "Jake, you should be more careful."

And I almost shouted, "Yeah, well, *you* should pay more attention. Don't you know there's a SuperBully loose in your classroom?"

But of course I didn't say that. Because the

second rule about bullies is that if you tattle to the teacher, things might get a lot worse. And I had a feeling things were going to be bad enough already.

And I was right.

CHAPTER THREE

# From Bad to Worse

So I got on the bus after Link's first day of school. I looked out the window. I saw Link walking behind Mrs. Brattle. She was showing him which bus to ride home.

"Please," I whispered. "Not my bus. Not bus three. Please, please, please, not bus three."

But Mrs. Brattle led him right over to bus number three. And ten seconds later, Link was on my bus, standing there next to me. Looking down at me.

In a voice much louder than it needed to be,

he said, "Hey, Fake, anyone else gonna sit here?"

I looked up and I remembered how tall he was. But now he was messing with my name. And he already had me mad and scared at the same time. But I didn't care, because I didn't want him to make fun of my name.

So I said, "My name's Jake, Jake Drake." And right away I knew I had made a mistake. Because now he knew that I cared about him goofing around with my name.

Link smiled that special bully-smile. He said, "Yeah, I know. Like I said. Your name's Fake, Fake Drake." And that made the other kids on the bus start laughing. And then he sat down next to me.

He didn't push me or hit me, because anybody can do that sort of thing. He was a new kind of bully. He was a SuperBully.

I felt my ears turning red. My lips were clamped together. I turned my head away from him and looked out the window. I was ready for the next attack.

But it didn't come. A fourth grader in the seat across had a baseball glove. So Link said, "What's the best Little League team in this town?"

And Link started talking about how he was on the top team in his old town. He didn't want to join a new team unless it was going to be a winner.

It was like I wasn't there. I was right there on the seat next to him, but I might as well have been on the moon.

The bus stopped at Maple Street, and some kids got off. Then at Cross Street, and more kids got off. And then the bus was at my stop, Greenwood Street.

So I said, "I have to get off at this stop." About ten kids stood up as the bus slowed down. But Link kept on talking to the fourth grader about Little League.

So I said it louder. "This is my stop. I have to get off here."

I looked over the seat in front of me. There were only three kids left, up by the bus driver.

So I shouted, "NOW. I have to get off NOW!"

The bus driver looked up into her mirror and frowned. But Link smiled at her. And loud enough for everyone to hear, he said, "Oops.

Almost forgot, Fake. I'm a new kid, remember? This is my stop, too. This is where me and Fake Drake get off the bus."

Following Link Baxter off the bus? That was one of the worst moments of my life. As I went down those tall black steps, I thought, *Every morning and every afternoon and all day long for the rest of second grade—maybe even for the rest of my life—it's going to be me and Link Baxter.*

Something was going to have to change.

CHAPTER FOUR

# Bullyitis

Link didn't even talk to me when I got off the bus. He just walked away. I watched him. He crossed Greenwood Street and started to walk down Park Street.

And then I remembered. Of course! Link had moved into the Carsons' old house. The house had been for sale, and now it was Link's house. Right on Park Street. Right around the corner from me.

When I walked into my house, I didn't even

say hi to my mom. I dropped my book bag on the floor. Then I went right to the playroom.

My little sister, Abby, was watching a puppet show on TV. It was her favorite show.

I said, "Give me that!" And I grabbed the remote from her. She frowned at me and stuck her tongue out. Then I changed the channel to *Batman*.

Abby said, "Hey! I'm watching my puppets."

And I said, "Oh, yeah?" And I went over to her. She was sitting on a big pillow on the floor. I felt a lot taller than Abby. I said, "Well, I'm watching *Batman*, and you can't stop me." Then I kicked her pillow.

Abby yelled, "Ow! Ow! That hurt! Mom, Jake stole the remote. And he just kicked me, HARD!"

Mom came in. She was walking her fast walk. That's her "You're in big trouble" walk.

She stopped and stood over me. She said, "Jake Drake, you know better than to come in here and make a fuss! You come right back to the kitchen and pick up your book bag. And give that remote back to your sister."

I tossed the remote to Abby. By mistake it hit her on the knee. "OWWW!" Now she really yelled, and she tried to cry a little too.

So real quick, I said, "Sorry." But I was too late. Mom took me by the arm and marched me to the kitchen.

She put me on a chair. Then she said, "Jake, we do not treat others like that in this family, and you know it! What's gotten into you!?"

And then it hit me. It was Link. Link had gotten into me! I was being like Link. I had caught BULLYITIS!

But I couldn't tell my mom about Link. Because my mom might call Link's mom. Then Link would tell every kid on the bus how Fake Drake went and cried to his mommy. And every day on the bus for the rest of my life I would hear about how I'm such a big baby.

So I said, "Sorry, Mom." Then I gave a big sigh. "I guess I'm just tired and hungry."

Moms love to hear that. Tired and hungry—that's stuff that moms know how to fix.

Mom patted me on the head. Then she fixed me a peanut butter sandwich and a glass of milk.

And she said, "I'll make sure you get to bed early tonight, sweetheart. But when that sandwich is gone, you have to go apologize to Abby."

So I ate slowly. But then I put my dish and my glass in the sink and went to look for Abby.

And I thought it was going to be like all the other times I had told Abby I was sorry.

But it wasn't.

CHAPTER FIVE

# What Abby Said

Abby was only in kindergarten back then—back when I was in second grade. Even so, Abby wasn't stupid like a lot of little kids are.

I'd never tell her this, but Abby's okay to talk to sometimes. You know, for a sister. I mean, since I don't have a dog or anything. Abby's kind of like a pet who can talk. Sort of like a parrot, I guess.

Anyway, I told Abby I was sorry.

"It's okay," she said.

See what I mean? How Abby's kind of like a

pet? You know how if you yell at a dog, it gets all scared of you, or maybe mad? But then you pat it on the head, and it starts wagging its tail again? That's the way Abby is.

She was still watching the puppets. They were painting some clouds on a wall. Really dumb.

Then I told Abby about Link.

And Abby said, "His sister came to school today. Linda Baxter. She's in kindergarten with me. She's a bully, too."

I said, "Really?"

"Yes," said Abby. "Linda took Sara's crayons. I saw."

Abby started moving her arms like the puppets.

I said, "So she took Sara's crayons?"

Abby nodded, only half listening. "Yes. The best colors. Linda said, 'If you tell, I'll break them.' At snack time Sara gave Linda a Ritz cracker. Then Linda let Sara use the yellow crayon."

So there it was. The Case of the Kidnapped Crayons.

And I said to myself, *Linda Baxter is only in* kindergarten*! Link's baby sister is already a SuperBully.* And then I thought, *Imagine what*

*her big brother is going to do to* me!

Not a good thought.

Abby kept watching the puppets. The show was almost over. The puppets were starting to sing. It's the part of the show that almost makes me throw up.

Then I remembered something. I remembered going to visit Gramma and Grampa in Florida. It was just me and Abby. And I was mad because I always had to do everything with Abby. She was just four. She was still in nursery school, and I was already a big first grader. I hated hanging around with such a baby. I was mean to Abby the whole time.

So I said, "Remember how I was mean to you when we went to Florida?"

Abby was nodding to the music. But she said, "I remember."

And I said, "How come you didn't get mad at me?"

Abby shrugged. "If I get mad, I feel mean. I don't like to feel mean. So I don't get mad."

Then Abby started to sing along with the puppets. I did not want to throw up, so I went to my room. I flopped onto my bed so I could think about my problems.

Part of me wished I could get a ride to school with Dad every morning. Then I wouldn't have to ride the bus with Link. And maybe I could go to the library for recess. And then Mom could pick me up after school.

Part of me wished I would grow ten inches in one night. Then tomorrow morning I would get on the bus. I would sit next to Link. I would push his face against the window. I would paint his nose with a red Magic Marker. I would call him Fink. Fink Baxter.

But I kept thinking. And Abby was right. It's not fun to feel mean. Link acted like it *was* fun. But it wasn't, really—was it? No. It couldn't be.

As I went to sleep that night, here's what I said to myself: *Tomorrow, I will not get mad at Link. No matter what. Then he will see that it's not fun to be mean.*

It worked for Abby and me.

But would it work for a SuperBully?

CHAPTER SIX

# Playing It Cool

In the morning, Link made sure that he sat next to me on the bus. First thing, he wiped mud from his shoes onto my book bag. But I just smiled and brushed it off. Very cool.

He called me Jake Flake. I laughed and said, "Yeah, that's a good one! Or how about Snake Drake? Or . . . Cheesecake Drake? Or maybe . . . maybe, Shaky Jake? Yeah, Shaky Jake."

Everybody on the bus laughed. But it was me making them laugh, not Link. I was playing it cool.

Link didn't like it. His beady little eyes got meaner and meaner. And when we got to school, he pushed his way up to the front so he got off the bus first. He even pushed some fifth graders.

In class it got worse. Link stuck some gum onto my math workbook. I just smiled and put a piece of paper over the sticky part. I kept working, cool as could be.

During art class Link poured some gold glitter into the paint I was using. I said, "Nice idea!" And I kept painting.

Later, the art teacher said, "Jake, I *love* what you've done there. Very creative."

Very creative, and very *cool.*

I was worried about recess. The playground is big. Anything can happen out there.

Sure enough, Link cut in line and got behind me on the sliding board. I slid down, and he came down behind me really fast. He tried to bump me into a puddle. But I stepped aside real fast, and his foot went into some mud.

It's a good thing Mrs. Brattle was standing so close. Otherwise, Link might have tried to make me lick that mud off his shoe or something.

After lunch I was in the boys' room washing my hands. I looked in the mirror, and there was Link. Smiling. I tried to smile back, but it was hard. I was scared.

Link kept smiling. He started to wash his hands at the sink next to me. And when I got a paper towel, he cupped his hands and threw a ton of water right at me. Right down the front of my tan pants. A big brown wet spot.

Then in this baby voice Link said, "Wook, wook! Wittle Jakey had a accident!" A bunch of fourth graders started pointing and laughing.

I tried to laugh, too. I tried to be cool, but I couldn't. I couldn't laugh. Not about that. I got angry. I felt like flames were going to shoot out of my eyes.

And Link saw. He saw me get mad. Then he saw me get even madder about him seeing me get mad. And Link's beady little eyes and his smirky little mouth laughed. At me.

I stayed in the boys' room as long as I could. I rubbed on my pants with paper towels. I fanned my pants with my hands. But when I went back to class, there was still a big dark spot.

And Link had been whispering. Everybody looked at me when I came in the door. My face turned bright pink. And when I sat down across from Link, he held his nose and made a face.

I couldn't help it. I was so mad. And it made me feel mean. And I lost it. I turned toward Link and I punched him on the shoulder with all my might.

Might is something I don't have a lot of. So I know I didn't really hurt him.

But Link was a lot better at acting than Abby. He grabbed his shoulder and knocked a book off his desk.

"Ahh!" he shouted. "Ahh! My arm, my arm!"

Mrs. Brattle was there in one second flat. "Jake! I am *ashamed* of you!"

Link let his arm flop down like it was broken. He whimpered, "Ahh, my arm, my arm! It hurts."

Mrs. Brattle said, "Ted, please help Link down to the nurse's office. And Jake, you come with me."

As Link left the room, he peeked a look back at me. And he smiled.

Link Baxter was off to get some ice and some friendly words from the nurse.

And me? I was off to talk with the principal—probably not a happy little chat. And my pants still had a big stain down the front.

Mrs. Brattle walked me down the hall. On the way, I figured something out. Link was a bigger problem than Abby had ever faced.

This was war, and I was losing. Big time.

Not cool. Not cool at all.

CHAPTER SEVEN

# Learning My Lesson

When people are mad at you, they do a lot of pointing. In the office, Mrs. Brattle pointed to a chair. She said, "Wait here." No smiles. Then she went into the principal's office.

A minute later she came out, and so did Mrs. Karp. Mrs. Karp pointed to her office and said, "In there, Jake."

I had never been to the principal's office before. There was a big gray desk. There was a row of big gray bookcases. And there was a big gray principal. Mrs. Karp had gray shoes, a gray

MS. KARP

dress, and gray hair. And she was taller than Mrs. Brattle. Even taller than my dad.

She pointed at a gray chair in front of her desk. "Sit there, Jake." So I sat down. Then she said, "You know it's against the rules to hit some-one, don't you." It wasn't a question.

And I said, "Yes, I know."

"Then why did you hit Link Baxter?"

This was the tricky part. If I told about Link being a bully, then I would be a tattletale. But if I didn't say *something*, then she would think I was some crazy hitter. So I pointed at the spot on my pants. And I said, "Some water got on my pants in the boys' room. And I thought Link was mak-ing fun."

So simple. So true. So easy for Mrs. Karp to understand. And she did. Just like that. She got a friendly look on her face and said, "I understand about feeling embarrassed, Jake. But do you see that hitting is wrong, no matter what?"

And I said, "Yes." Because it was true. I really was sorry I had hit Link. I did not want to have a fight with Link. Ever. For two reasons.

First, because it's not good to hit and kick

and scratch and pull hair and roll around on the ground. And second, because I knew what would happen to me if I ever *did* get in a fight with Link. I would turn into one huge purple bruise.

So Mrs. Karp sent me back to my classroom. She didn't even call my mom.

As she opened the door to her office for me she said, "I'm sure you've learned your lesson, haven't you, Jake?"

And I said, "Yes, Mrs. Karp." Only I didn't know if we were talking about the same lesson.

As I walked from the school office toward Mrs. Brattle's room, Link came out of the nurse's office. I think he had been waiting for me. He walked beside me. In the empty hallway Link seemed bigger than ever.

He gave me that bully-smile and said, "Nice move, Flake. Have a good time with the principal?"

This was the first time I had been alone with Link. I was scared, but I said, "It wasn't so bad." We kept walking.

Being alone with Link was different. And I thought that maybe a bully stops being a bully if there aren't some other kids around to watch. I thought that maybe he's only a SuperBully when he has an audience. For a second, it felt like Link Baxter was just this big kid, and I was walking down the hall with him.

Back then I didn't know as much about bullies as I do now. So I said, "How come you pick on me?"

Wrong question. The SuperBully was back. Link looked at me like I was a bug. He said, "Dumb question." And I thought maybe he was going to push me into a locker or something.

But he didn't. And we just kept walking.

But it was like my question confused him. And just before we got back to room twenty-three, I knew. I knew why he didn't answer the question.

He didn't because he *couldn't*. He couldn't tell me why because he didn't really know.

But there had to be a reason why Link was a bully.

And if I could figure out that reason—or if I could give him a reason NOT to be a bully—then Link Baxter, SuperBully, would become Link Baxter, *Ex*-SuperBully.

CHAPTER EIGHT

# Dangerous Duo

The next week was not fun.

Every chance he got, Link did something mean. Like step on my red pen and break it. Or something embarrassing. Like push me into a bunch of fourth-grade girls in the cafeteria. Or something annoying. Like hide my book bag under the seats at the back of the bus.

I was starting to think that Link was a bully because Link was a bully. And I was starting to think there was nothing I could do about it. Except live with it. Every day. For the rest of my life.

Just when I was sure things could not get worse, they did. Thanks to Mrs. Brattle.

Thanksgiving was coming, and we all had to do a social studies project about it. Mrs. Brattle planned all the topics. And Mrs. Brattle wanted everyone to work in pairs. And Mrs. Brattle chose the pairs. And one pair was Jake Drake and Link Baxter. We had to do a report to show how the Native Americans had lived.

Link loved it. He thought it was so funny. A big joke.

He said, "Hey, Flake. This is great. It's you and me. We get to make a teepee together. Tell you what. I'll do the tee part, and you can take care of the pee. Get it? The *pee?*"

Of course, I wanted to tell Link how dumb he was! Because the Native Americans at the first Thanksgiving never saw a teepee. They lived in wetu, round wigwams made of poles and bark. And they made longhouses, too. But you don't say things like that to a SuperBully.

I went up to Mrs. Brattle when everyone else

went to lunch. I said, "Mrs. Brattle, I don't think I should work with Link on the Thanksgiving project."

She said, "Oh? Why is that?"

"Well," I said, "I just think I'd do better with someone else."

Mrs. Brattle said, "I'm sorry, but everyone else is already paired up, Jake. I'm sure you and Link will do just fine."

On the bus home that day, Link said, "That Thanksgiving thing? You're going to do the report, Flake. I don't do dumb stuff like that."

I said, "What do you mean? We're partners."

Link said, "Yeah, right. And you're the partner who has to do the report."

The next day we had library period. I watched Link. He went right to the reference section. He got the *N* encyclopedia. *Good*, I thought. *He's going to look up things about the Native Americans.* Link carried the encyclopedia to a table at the back of the library. My partner was working. Looked good to me.

ENCYCLOPEDIA
N

I went to find some other stuff about Native Americans in Massachusetts.

Near the end of the period I went to show Link the books I found.

He looked up and said, "Great job, Flake."

I said, "What did you find?"

And he said, "Take a look." Behind the encyclopedia Link was reading a book of Garfield cartoons. He said, "I love social studies, don't you?"

So there it was: My partner wasn't just a SuperBully. He was also a moron.

Then it was the day before the project was due.

I had found all the books. I had found all the pictures. I had used my best handwriting to make some labels. I had stuff I could tell about, but we still didn't have a project or anything to show the class.

At the end of the day, Mrs. Brattle said, "Remember, all the Thanksgiving projects are due tomorrow."

So after we got off the bus that afternoon, Link came up to me. He said, "Hey, Flake. Did you finish that dumb report yet?"

And I said, "No. We still have to make something to show about the Native Americans."

And he said, "Well, you better finish it tonight."

It was the way he said it. Like he could just order me around. He thought he could just look at me and make me do whatever he wanted me to. But I was tired of doing all the work. It wasn't fair.

Something inside me snapped. And I said, "No. I'm not going to."

Link took a step closer. He said, "What?"

"I said I'm not going to. I don't care what you say or what you do. I'm not going to make a wigwam or anything else by myself. And if you don't help, then I guess we're just going to get an F on our report."

Link looked down at me with his beady little bully eyes. He clenched his fists. For a second I thought I had made a big mistake. I was about to get pounded into the sidewalk.

Then suddenly, he shrugged. He said, "Fine. Okay. Come over to my house about three-thirty. We'll make a stupid poster or something."

Then he just turned and started walking home.

Standing there in the November sunshine at the corner of Greenwood and Park, I felt like something had changed. It didn't feel like I had killed a dragon or anything.

It was more like back when I was five. Every night I'd thought there was a monster under my bed. And then one night I'd gotten brave enough to look. And it wasn't there. No monster.

But in forty-five minutes I was going to have to go knock on Link's door. Who would open it?

Would it be my social studies partner?

Or a monster?

CHAPTER NINE

# Surprises and Questions

Finding Link's house was no problem. He lived in Jimmy Carson's old house, and I had been there plenty of times. I had all the stuff for the project in my book bag.

I went up the front steps and rang the doorbell. I heard a sound. From above. Like *shhhh.*

I looked up just in time to see a fat red water balloon. And above the balloon, Link's head, sticking out of a window on the second floor.

The balloon went *SPLAT* on the steps next to me. Only my shoes got wet. Link laughed and yelled, "Surprise!" Then he said, "Come on in, Flake. Door's open."

My heart was pounding, and I almost turned around and ran for home.

But I didn't. If Link had wanted to put that balloon right on my head, he could have. So that was progress, right? Or was he really trying to soak me, and he just missed?

Anyway, I went inside.

Link's mom was in the front hallway looking through a stack of mail. She must have just gotten home, because her coat was still on. She smiled and said, "Hi. You must be Jake. Link said you were coming over to work on a project. If you get hungry later, you can have a snack."

I said, "Thank you."

Link yelled from the top of the stairs, "Hey! Up here. And bring all your stuff."

Link's room was a surprise. I guess I'd thought it would be like a cave or jail cell or something. It was just a regular room.

There were a lot of comic books around, and there were models on all the shelves. Lots of them. Model cars and trucks and motorcycles. Model ships and airplanes. Even a model train.

I picked up a model of a car.

"Hey! Hands off, Flake."

I put the car down. But I bent over to get a better look.

It was perfect. It was only a plastic model, like the kind at a hobby shop. It had been glued together and then painted bright blue. Perfectly.

I looked at Link. He had flopped onto his bed. He was looking at an *X-Men* comic book.

I said, "This is cool. Where'd you get it?"

"My dad gave me the kit. It's a 1969 Ford Mustang convertible."

I said, "You mean *you* put it together?"

"Yeah," said Link. He didn't take his eyes off the comic book. "I painted it, too."

I could imagine Link having a hobby like collecting wrestling cards. Or catching bugs and spiders. Or maybe throwing glass bottles against a brick wall. But model building? Link?

A girl wearing sweatpants and a green T-shirt came into Link's room. She was tall, with big shoulders and arms, probably in high school. She had about six earrings in each ear, and her hair was brown with a bright pink streak in the front. And she was mad.

She didn't notice me. Real loud, she said, "Hey, Stink."

Link looked up from his comic book. "What?"

"You know what. You took a dollar off my dresser this morning."

"Did not!"

She picked up the Mustang model I had been looking at. She held it out, and started to close her big hand around it.

Link sat up and yelled, "Hey, leave that alone."

She smiled, and her smile looked very familiar to me. Then she said, "Here—catch!" and she tossed the model at Link.

Link caught it before it hit the bed.

The girl said, "I *know* you took that dollar."

Link said, "You probably spent all your money on lipstick or something dumb. And you're so stupid, you probably don't even remember."

She took two steps into the room. "Yeah well,

see if you can remember this, Stink. If I *ever* find you in my room, you are dead." Then she looked at me. "And that goes for your twerpy little friends, too."

Then she left. A few seconds later, a door slammed. Hard.

Link grinned at me and reached over and put the model on the table by his bed. "That's my demented sister."

I got out the book that had some pictures of a Native American village. I was ready to finish this project and go home. Giant girl SuperBullies are not my idea of fun. I said, "Let's get this done, okay?"

Link heaved a bored sigh. "Yeah, okay. I've got some stuff we can use."

He rolled off the bed and walked to a table near the window. There was a big box. It was the kind of box you get new clothes in at Christmas. He pulled off the lid. "We can make something on the inside of this lid."

I said, "Okay."

But I was looking at the things in the box.

There were some brown paper bags, and some sticks and twigs. There were some plastic bags full of sand, and some pieces of dried moss. There were bunches of long green pine needles. And there was some string and some glue.

There was also a page that Link must have ripped out of a *National Geographic* magazine. It showed a painting of a Wampanoag village, complete with wigwams and a longhouse. He had actually done some research.

Link said, "I got most of this junk from my backyard."

"Oh," I said. "So your idea is to make a model village? And to make it look real?"

He looked at me. "Duh. Good thinking, Flake."

I picked up one of the longer sticks. "This could be one of the wigwam poles."

Link shook his head. "Too thick. I got these skinny sticks for that. If they're not skinny, it won't look right."

For the next hour I watched Link work. I tried to help, but I just got in the way.

First Link bent seven or eight skinny sticks to

make a wigwam frame. He tied the sticks together with part of an old shoelace. Then he cut open a big brown bag with scissors. He ripped the brown paper into ragged pieces. He painted little lines all over them. They looked like tree bark. Then he glued the paper onto the wigwam frame.

I showed Link one of the books I brought. He rubbed some black marker onto a paper towel. Then he rubbed that onto the brown paper to make the wigwam look old. Then he glued the whole thing in the box lid.

Then he spread some sand and moss around. He used big stones to look like rocks. He made a little fireplace outside the wigwam with a ring of pebbles. And he used wood and crumpled foil and a red marker to make the fire look real. He made trees and bushes out of the pine needles. And then he made another smaller wigwam. And then he made a longhouse.

It was amazing. It looked like a little village. It looked so good.

Link put down the glue bottle and stepped back a few feet.

I said, "It's really great."

Link shrugged. "It's okay."

I put my things back in my book bag and pulled on my coat. "So you'll bring it to school tomorrow?"

Link snorted. "You think I'm going to let you carry it? And trip and fall all over the place like a doofus? I'll bring it."

I said, "Okay. So I'll see you tomorrow."

Link flopped back onto his bed and picked up another comic book. "Yeah. So long, Flake." Then he said, "Hey, don't forget, Flake. You better do a good job giving this report."

But by then I was halfway down the hall. I tiptoed past his big sister's room and went downstairs. I opened the door, stuck my head out, and looked up. No Link, no water balloons. So I scooted across the steps and headed for home.

I had some stuff I needed to think about.

I had seen a lot at Link's house.

Like his big sister. What would it be like to live in the same house with *that* your whole life?

And his mom. She seemed nice.

And then there was Link.

Sure, he water-bombed me, and he ignored me a lot, and he called me a doofus. But he didn't seem like a SuperBully, at least not all the time. Once in a while, he was just—well, he was just like a kid.

And he was absolutely a great model builder.

I had looked at Link's face while he was thinking about the model. And while he was painting and gluing. When he forgot I was there, he had a different face from his bully face. Not mean. Almost nice.

But when Link remembered I was there, his face would switch back.

So if there's no one to bully, a bully isn't a bully, right?

I couldn't make myself disappear.

But could I make a SuperBully disappear?

That was the question I still could not answer.

CHAPTER TEN

# Busted Link

Link wasn't on the bus the next morning. His dad drove him to school with the project.

Right after math in the morning, Mrs. Brattle said, "Now we're going to look at the Thanksgiving projects. First, you should show what you made, and then tell why it's part of the first Thanksgiving story."

Andrea and Laura went first. They had made a poster to show the inside of the *Mayflower*. It looked like their parents had done most of the drawing. And they both talked too soft and giggled a lot.

Then Ben and Carlos showed Plymouth Rock. It was where the Pilgrims had landed. The rock was made of papier-mâché. Except they didn't use enough paint. You could still see the comics and the headlines on the strips of newspaper. But it was an okay report.

And then Mrs. Brattle said, "Jake, Link? You're going to tell us something about the Native Americans."

I said, "Our project is out in the hall under the coatrack."

Link followed me out into the hall. There was a white plastic bag covering the project. The sand and rocks made the box lid heavy. I picked up one end, and Link got the other end. We started toward the door.

Then Link stopped. His face looked pale, and his lips looked blue. In a small voice he said, "I can't do this. Reports. You know, talking to the whole class." He gulped. And then very softly he said, "I can't."

We were face-to-face, about two feet apart. I

was looking up at him. No SuperBully in sight. Just a scared kid. And then I knew why Link had kept telling me that I had to give the report.

Then I felt this rush of power. At last, the great and fearsome Link—completely at my mercy! At last, it was my turn to be the bulliest SuperBully of all!

I could have said, "Oh, wook! It's Wittle Winky—afwaid of a weport!"

I could have said, "So—you make me feel terrible for a whole month, and now you want me to feel sorry for you? Well, too bad, tough guy!"

Or I could have said, "Hurry—let's get in the room so the whole class can see mighty Link Baxter throw up all over the floor—ha, ha, ha!"

But I didn't.

I said, "It'll be okay. Really. All you have to do is stand there and point at stuff when I talk about it. This is a great model. Everyone's going to think it's the best."

Link swallowed hard and took a deep breath. "Okay . . . but you're gonna do the report, right?"

I nodded, and we carried the project into the room and up to the table by the chalkboard.

I looked at a card I had made and said, "We made something to show how the Native Americans lived before the Pilgrims came."

And Link pulled the bag off the model. Some kids in the back stood up so they could see it better. And Mrs. Brattle said, "Everyone should come up closer so you can see. This is really special. Careful, don't bump the table."

The kids were blown away. And so was I. Because after I left his house the day before, Link made some more stuff. He made little bows and arrows. He made some spears and some little baskets, and the baskets had little yellow beads in them, yellow like the color of corn.

So I said, "This is what part of a village looked like. The wigwams and longhouses were made of poles covered with tree bark."

I kept talking, and Link pointed at things. He didn't look like he was going to be sick anymore.

When I was done telling about everything, I said, "And I have to tell the truth. This whole thing? Link made it, and planned it, and he did all the painting, too. I helped a little, but really, Link made it."

And the kids all clapped, and so did Mrs. Brattle. Link's face got red, but he smiled. And it wasn't a bully-smile. It was his real smile.

On the bus home that afternoon, Link sat next to me. But it was different. He didn't poke me or grab my book bag. He just sat there. Like a kid. He joked around with some fourth graders.

When we got off at our stop, I turned toward my house and he turned toward his. But before I turned the corner, he called out, "Hey!"

I cringed. I couldn't help it. It sounded like Link's bully-voice.

He trotted over. No bully-face. He said, "What you did at school today? Thanks." Then he looked all embarrassed. He shrugged and said, "See ya later, Jake."

And I said, "Yeah. See ya."

Then it hit me. Link didn't call me Flake, or Fake. He called me Jake.

So now I'm in fourth grade. And Link still lives around the corner from me. He's even bigger now. I think he might start shaving soon.

It's not like we became best friends or anything. He still pretty much thinks I'm a dweeb. And I still pretty much think he's a moron. We never worked on another project together.

And it's not like Link stopped being a bully. But he did stop being a SuperBully. And he never bullied me again. Ever.

I'm still kind of small for my age, still the perfect size for bullying, and I still look kind of smart, and I haven't turned into a tattletale. But if a kid starts to bully me now, it never lasts. I know too much. Bullies don't fool me anymore. Because back behind those mean eyes and that bully-face, there's another face. A real face.

And if I keep looking for that real face, I see it. And the bully sees me see it.

And *BAM*, just like that, another bully gets busted.

By me. Jake Drake, Bully Buster.

# What's next for Jake Drake?

Here's a look at what happens when
Jake's science project turns him
into a Know-It-All.

CHAPTER ONE

# The Catch

I'm Jake, Jake Drake. I'm in fourth grade, and I'm ten years old. And I have to tell the truth about something: I've been crazy about computers all my life.

My first computer was an old Mac Classic with a black-and-white screen. I got to play Reader Rabbit and Magic Math. I got to draw pictures on the screen, and I played Battle Tanks. And that was before I could even read.

Then our family got a Mac with a big color

monitor. And I got to play Tetris and Shanghai and Solitaire and Spectre. Then I got a joystick for Christmas when I was four, and so did my best friend, Willie. Whenever Willie came to my house we played computer games together. It's not like we played computers all the time, because my mom made a one-hour-a-day rule at my house. But Willie and I filled up that hour almost every day.

Then the computers started getting super-fast, and I started messing around with Virtual Drummer, and then SimCity, and SimAnt, and PGA Golf, and about ten other games. And then the Internet arrived at my house, and all of a sudden I could make my computer do some pretty amazing stuff. It was like a magic window.

I'm telling all of this because if I don't, then the rest of this story makes me look like a real jerk. And I'm not a jerk, not most of the time. I just really like computers.

When I started kindergarten, there was a computer in our room. When the teacher saw I was good on it, I got to use it. I even got to teach other kids how to use it. Except for Kevin and

Marsha. They didn't want me to tell them about computers or anything else.

Like I said before, I'm ten now, so I've had some time to figure out some stuff. And one thing I know for sure is this: There's nothing worse than a know-it-all.

Don't get me wrong. I'm pretty smart, and I like being smart. And almost all the kids I know, they're pretty smart, too.

But some kids, they have to prove they're smart. Like, all the time. And not just smart. They have to be the smartest. And that's what Marsha and Kevin are like.

Marsha McCall and Kevin Young were nice enough kids back in kindergarten—as long as I didn't try to tell them anything about the computer. Because when I tried to show Kevin how to make shapes with the drawing program, he said, "I know that." But I don't think he really did. And when I tried to show Marsha how to print out a picture of a kitten, she said, "I can do that myself."

But a lot of the time Kevin and Marsha were pretty nice because kindergarten was mostly playtime.

But when we got to first grade, school

changed. All of a sudden there were right answers and wrong answers. And Kevin and Marsha, they went nuts about getting the right answers.

But it was worse than that. They both wanted to get the right answer *first.* It was like they thought school was a TV game show. If you get the right answer first, you win the big prize. Anyway, they both turned into know-it-alls.

Our first-grade teacher was Miss Grimes. Every time she asked a question, Marsha would start shaking all over and waving her hand around and whispering really loud, like this: "Ooh, ooh! I know! I know! I know!"

And while Marsha was going, "Ooh, ooh," Kevin looked like his arm was going to pull his whole body right out of his chair and drag it up to the ceiling, like his arm had its own brain or something.

It was pretty awful. But Miss Grimes, she liked it when Kevin and Marsha tried to be the best at everything. She liked seeing who could get done first with a math problem. She liked letting everyone with a hundred on a spelling quiz line up first for lunch or recess. First grade felt like a big contest, and Miss Grimes smiled at the winners and frowned at the losers.

When she asked the class a question, most of the time Miss Grimes called on Marsha first. If Marsha was slow or didn't know something, then Kevin got a turn. If Kevin messed up, then she would call on someone else.

And I think I know why Miss Grimes always called on Marsha and Kevin. I think it's because she's kind of a know-it-all herself. I bet she was just like Marsha back when she was in first grade.

Second grade wasn't much better. The only good thing was that my second-grade teacher wasn't like Miss Grimes. Mrs. Brattle didn't want school to be a big contest. So she hardly ever called on the know-it-alls.

All year long, Mrs. Brattle kept saying stuff like, "Kevin and Marsha, please look around at all the other students in this class. They have good ideas, too. Just put your hands down for now."

That didn't stop Kevin and Marsha. The "ooh-oohing" and the arm waving never let up.

But last year, when I was in third grade, that's

when things got out of control. And I guess it was partly my fault.

And Mrs. Snavin, my third-grade teacher? She had something to do with it. And so did the principal, Mrs. Karp.

And so did this guy named Mr. Lenny Cordo over at Wonky's Super Computer Store. He had *a lot* to do with it.

Because Mr. Lenny Cordo came to my school one day back when I was in third grade. And Mr. Lenny Cordo told me that he had a present for me. Something really wonderful. Something I had been wishing for.

But there was one small catch. Because there's always at least one small catch.

And this was the catch: Before Mr. Lenny Cordo could give me this wonderful thing that I wanted so much, I would have to do something.

I would have to turn myself into Jake Drake, Know-It-All.